Leafing Through the Seasons

A collection of stories and poems from
Northumbria Region u3a Creative
Writers' Group

Published in 2022 by FeedARead.com Publishing
Copyright © The authors named within the publication.

The authors assert their moral right under the Copyright, Designs and Patents Act, 1988, to be identified as the author of their individual work.

All Rights reserved. No part of this publication may be reproduced, copied, stored in a retrieval system, or transmitted, in any form or by any means, without the prior written consent of the copyright holder, nor be otherwise circulated in any form of binding or cover other than that in which it is published and without a similar condition being imposed on the subsequent purchaser.

A CIP catalogue record for this title is available from the British Library.

ACKNOWLEGEMENTS

Spring Sketch
https://pixabay.com

Summer Sketch
https://publicdomainvectors.org/en/search/summer/4

Autumn Sketch
https://publicdomainvectors.org/en/search/acorns

Winter Sketch
https://publicdomainvectors.org/en/search/snowflake

Foreword

'Learn, laugh, live'

The u3a is pleased to be celebrating its 40th anniversary. The Northumbria Region u3a Creative Writers' Group is delighted to mark this special year with our collection of stories and poems.

Founded in 1982, u3a is a UK-wide movement of locally run interest groups that provide a wide range of opportunities for members to explore new ideas, skills and activities together.

u3a has members who draw upon their own knowledge and experience, in a wide variety of subjects, to teach and learn from each other. There are no qualifications to pass – it is just for pleasure. Learning is its own reward.

There are 1,057 u3as in the UK, each a charity in its own right, with over 388,000 members. It is open to everyone who's no longer in full-time employment.

In the Northumbria Region there are 49 individual u3as, with a membership of over 8,000 from Berwick u3a in Northumberland down to Saltburn u3a in North Yorkshire and many in between.

The Northumbria Region u3a Creative Writing Group started in February 2021, during the many lockdowns of the COVID pandemic. The Group consists of members from around the Region. Zoom was the only way all members could meet on a monthly basis.

As the 12 Creative Writing Groups throughout the Region began getting together after the pandemic, some original Zoom members went back to their own Creative Writing Groups. However, the Northumbria Region u3a Creative Writing Group, there are 14 members at the present time, still continues to meet on Zoom, with the occasional face to face social event.

The money raised from this first collection of short stories and poems will enable a workshop to be organised for all Creative Writing Groups in the Northumbria Region.

Cecilia Coulson.

Group Leader of the Northumbria Region u3a Creative Writers' Group
Chair of Northumbria Region u3a Committee

For further details about all u3as in the Northumbria Region u3a please look at the website www.u3asites.org.uk/northumbria

Seasonal Joy

Pauline Bennett

Spring

Tiny leaves unfurl

Holding the promise of joy.

Treachery lies close.

Summer

Heat enfolds, flora

Languidly metamorphose

Into bronze nectar.

Autumn

Earth slows her rhythm.

Ripe wealth must now be hidden.

Treasure in dark days.

Winter

Frost and Ice fine tune

Their bitter melody, Death

Stalks the hapless few.

.....

SPRING

awakening bud

spirit and lifeforce

bloom for our children.

Caroline Davison

Spring Lambs

Pat Atkinson

It's always a pleasure to look forward to Spring, to lighter, brighter days but beware of the saying *'March should come in like a lion and go out like a lamb'*.

In the past my husband and I nursed weakling new-born lambs when our kitchen became, not SCBU* but SCLU. After long and unpredictable lambing sessions cardboard boxes and washing baskets were utilised for neo-natal cribs in the hope that the warmth of the Aga and a little TLC would revive them. After being tube fed and tucked up in old jumpers and laid on a bed of straw my husband would say 'there you go, little lambie, you have two choices now.' (to live or die). Absolute joy made us beam with delight when a sudden, faint bleating emanated suggesting the choice was to live. Some of the surviving second chancers could be returned to their biological mother or adopted by another ewe by means of deception. The remainder were 'pet lambs' who grew up in the nursery field adjacent to our bungalow and needed time consuming bottle feeding at first until they could manage the adopter unit, principally a milk can with a circle of teats positioned at lamb height.

Now here's the strangest thing, when our daughter Jane was three months old, she cried for her feed just like a lamb and the pet lambs would come to the fence when they heard her. I feel very privileged to have witnessed such empathy.

*SCBU - Special Care Baby Unit

Trees

Caroline Davison

'Eat your carbon and you'll grow up to be big and strong.'

I know this speech off by heart, having heard it spoken to my siblings prior to every ceremony over the last Millennium. Today is the turn of another 'branch of the family'…..my Mother's ancient joke, yet it still makes the youngsters rustle with giggles.

Both parents will hold the forest spellbound with a quiet authority bestowed on them through a mixture of physical presence and their many years on the planet. Even the foolish treat them with respect. This is a special day for them and for every living being.

I watch with pride as my tiny cousins are gently transported from their nursery to
the outside world. First, they will feel the cold, damp, earth pressing into their bark, followed by the rush of adrenaline as freedom beckons.

A pompous dignitary will talk about 'capturing the air and filtering out impurities' trying to push all thoughts of lost profit from his mind, while our new green ambassadors simply marvel at the world around them.

Well hidden from ceremonial duties are our mischievous woodland creatures, soon they will pop up here and there, distracting, funny, just happy to be alive.

A naughty Red Squirrel will try and make my cousins laugh, hanging from a nearby branch and shaking his furry booty. Then there will be slow moving bands of earth hiding curious snouts and twitching whiskers. Camouflaged bodies squeezed together on logs, straining to see the new arrivals.

I feel my Father's wisdom within me, circles of knowledge and pain, enlightenment and hope. The canopy slowly dips and folds around us, a reflex action borne of experience.

'Today my children you represent our human's future, their hopes and dreams, our duty is to guide them and protect them, give them the green shoots of recovery they so badly need'.

His voice fuses past and present, even the pompous one can feel a change, experience a subtle movement ……but only confusion shows on his face.

While those who have an open channel to the Forest can hear quite clearly and the wonder on their faces fills my heart with love.

Make no mistake, these souls have long been derided as 'tree huggers' and 'plant whisperers', they felt the whip of humiliation for their beliefs.

Not anymore.

Now their expertise is sought after, now their opinions are listened to with avid interest. The intensity of the moment reaches into their hearts.

'Always remember those who dwell with Mother nature now outnumber the slow witted; they return our love, knowing our survival is mutual. An understanding has been forged. We will give them the strength they need to fight and win. They will increase our numbers and leave us to grow and thrive.'

The sing song voice of the forest rises to a crescendo and every heart now beats on a lighter note, every mind turns to renewal, every green shoot is a hero, as we hold the hand of spring.

.....

A Spring Haiku

Anita Langham

Cold gold stare on
Blue water forget-me-not
An emerald frog

.....

A Bit of Deja Vu

Maureen Taylor

'It sounds like a sewing machine with bronchitis', said my dad, as we watched Davy's old motorbike stagger round the corner. We wouldn't normally have been watching through the curtains like that, but we'd already heard it coming along the bottom road. I was holding my breath and clenching my fists. In my mind's eye, I could see it barely managing to crawl up the hill, being overtaken by next door's boys on their bikes. My Dad just shook his head and huffed. I don't know what he thought was the worst - me going out with a boy, me going out with a boy who rode a motorbike, or me going out with a boy who rode a wreck of a motorbike. He probably didn't know either. Pick your choose, as my mum used to say when there wasn't much choice at all.

I didn't care, though. To me, Davy was just all warm brown eyes and softness. He was different from the rest of the crowd. He had the bike so that he could get to college, and to the market where he had his part time job at the butcher's. But my Dad couldn't see those things. He just saw the leathers and a heap of junk on wheels.

Davy had promised to bring my mum something, and I hoped against hope it was going to be flowers from the stall next door, and not chops or mince. My heart was in my mouth when he reached inside his studded jacket and pulled out a squashed-up bunch of bedraggling tulips. My

mum looked really pleased but I thought a pound of mince might have been better after all.

My Dad pulled himself up to his best 5' 9" and extended his hand to Davy. Davy accepted, but he hadn't yet taken off his thick leather glove. It was a pity he didn't take his helmet off either as I knew his brown eyes would really have sealed it, even my Dad would have melted a bit. I saw my Dad roll his eyes at my mum, but she looked at my Dad square and said,

'I'll have to try to remember where I put the flower vase - it's that long since I've needed it.' and off she clipped into the kitchen.

'I want you back by 11, mind,' my dad said as we were leaving.

'Don't wait up', I wanted to say as I climbed onto the back of the bike, wrapping my arms around Davy's waist, breathing in the scent of his leather jacket.

We started courting in the May, and we had a great summer together. I did really like Davy, but soon it was time for him to go off to University (yes, a lad from round our way going to University). We decided that it would be better to finish and get on with our separate lives. I was still working at the Bakery, of course, and maybe I thought I wouldn't be good enough for him, being that he was going to be a professional with a career, not just a job like the rest of us.

I did think about Davy a lot at first, but then life takes over, doesn't it? And it wasn't long before I got in with Tom. He was so smooth, he even got on the good side of my Dad for a bit. And by Christmas we were married with Julie on the way. That's when you realise that everything in the garden isn't roses. I stuck it out for a long time, kidding myself that it was best for the girls. You do what you think is best at the time, don't you? Well, that's what we keep telling ourselves to drown out the truth our hearts are shouting in our ears.

They say 'what goes around comes around' and it was because of breaking up with Tom that I met Davy again, after all that time. Working in the solicitor's in town, smart suit, nice tie, same brown eyes. We couldn't meet up when he was working on the divorce, of course, but when it was all over, we did get together for a coffee. And, history repeating itself, here I am waiting in the front room for him to come and pick me up for our second first date. This time, Julie is by my side.

'Have you got your phone. mum? If you feel uncomfortable, you go to the bar and ask for Angela. They'll know what to do to keep you safe. Maybe it would have been better just to meet him in town? I could have come down with you on the bus and sat near. He wouldn't need to know I was there.'

She was out dadding my Dad, but maybe she is just better at saying feelings.

This time, there wasn't the sound of a bronchitic old motorbike coughing three streets away. Davy's got an

electric car that doesn't make a sound as it comes around the corner. The first we hear is the knock at the door. And what do you know, he's brought Julie a bunch of tulips, and he promises we'll be back by 11.

I link his arm as we walk down the path, and this time, I can say 'Don't wait up'

.....

Swan Song

Shirley Fall

Winter's swan song has come upon us,

Cloaking yellows in shrouds of white;

Daffodils hang their heads, heavy;

Forsythia's golden plumage stands out;

Coloured primulas cower under bushes' edge;

Intermittent sleety showers are punctuated

With bursts of brightness,

Streaking shadows of blue across the white of lawn-

Winter's swan song, a semicolon into Spring.

SUMMER

symphony of light

under your spell we flourish

narrator of life

Caroline Davison

The Jubilee Street Party

Susan Willis

Alice pulled her white cardigan over the blue dress she'd chosen to wear. She moaned as young Ellie appeared in the doorway to her room with a wheelchair.

'Oh no,' Alice mumbled, 'I hate going out in this thing!'

Ellie grinned and winked. 'Come on, stop bellyaching and get in the chair,' she said. 'You know it's too far to walk down to the party.'

Alice tutted but grinned at Ellie. She was her favourite carer in the home. All the others were nice and very kind, but Ellie teased and made her laugh. They had the same sense of humour which Alice loved.

When they got through the main doors and out into the fresh air Alice smiled then looked up into a blue sky. 'How lucky are we that the weather is so good for the street party?'

Ellie set off pushing her at a brisk pace which she also loved. The other carers treat her with kid-gloves because she was eighty-six which often irked Alice. She didn't feel her age and never had done. In her mind, she was still in her 60's but had to concede that her body hadn't kept up with her way of thinking.

They reached the library in no time and turned onto the long street in front of the town hall. Alice felt a bubble of excitement at the sight before her. Union Jack bunting stretched across the street from one lamppost to another. Kids were running around chasing balloons and a loudspeaker in the corner belted out popular music. There was a carefree euphoric atmosphere amongst everyone. Old pasting-tables meant for wallpaper had been covered with red, white, and blue plastic cloths. There were garden chairs and stools placed at the tables for all the families and other residents from her nursing home. Paper plates held meat and tuna sandwiches with bowls of crisps and nuts. There were big chocolate cakes sliced, small cup-cakes with fruit on the top, and slices of her favourite Battenburg cake. Alice licked her lips.

'Do you want to eat now,' Ellie asked.

Alice shook her head. 'Not just yet,' she said. 'I just want to soak it all in.'

'Yeah,' Ellie said. 'Everyone is in a good mood because they've got an extra bank holiday.' She secured the brakes on the wheelchair and bent forwards. 'Can you remember the last street party, Alice?'

She nodded. 'Oh, yes, but I remember the coronation street party more because it's where I met my Jim. It was on Tuesday 2nd June 1953, and we were both eighteen.'

Ellie whistled between her teeth. 'I bet you were a stunner?'
Alice smiled. 'Well, I did have a couple of lads chasing after me, but I never gave them a second look once I met

Jim. He was so handsome, and I knew at once that he was the one for me. We went to the cinema and after four months we got married.'

Ellie asked, 'So, did you watch the coronation on TV that day?'

Alice shook her head gently; the youngsters nowadays had no idea. 'No, we didn't have a TV set, Ellie. My family didn't have enough money to buy one, but we saw photographs of the queen who looked beautiful. Me and my girlfriends swooned over her dress and hoped she'd be a good queen. I remember the day like it was yesterday,' she said wistfully. 'When the king died, we weren't sure whether the young princess could step up to the mark. But she did and I'll be the first one to admit she's been good for the country.'

Alice's eyes misted over with the memories. She pulled out a white lace handkerchief from her sleeve and dabbed her eyes just in time to see a young man approach them. He was tall, slim with brown curly hair.

Wearing a short-sleeved T-Shirt, Alice noticed a tattoo on his arm of a heart with capital letters inside, E&K. She knew Ellie's boyfriend was called, Kyle and put two and two together.

He beamed at Ellie and Alice felt a pull on her heart strings. It was how Jim used to grin at her when he was trying to get in her good books and wanted something. Not that he'd asked for much in life. Jim had always been content just to be with her. And after a few years together she could finish his sentences because she knew him so well.

She sighed and looked up at Ellie who hadn't been her usual bubbly self since the weekend. Alice raised an eyebrow. Hmmm, she thought and knew there was something amiss. Had they had a tiff?

'Hey, there, Ellie,' he said. 'How's things?'

Alice watched Ellie stiffen her shoulders in the white uniform tunic. 'We're fine,' she said. 'This is Alice, who I've told you about.'

The young man swung towards Alice and smiled. 'Ahh, so you're the lady who Ellie talks about all the time,' he said. 'It's nice to meet you at long last.'

Alice smiled back up at him from the wheelchair. 'Hello, and you must be Kyle, who Ellie talks about all of the time, too.'

They both laughed but she noticed Ellie stare down at her black shoes. Yep, Alice thought, there's definitely something not right between them.

Ellie crossed her arms over her chest and Alice knew she was being huffy with him. 'We're just going to have something to eat,' Ellie said, releasing the break on the wheelchair.
She began to push Alice slowly towards the end of the table where there was a wide space next to the other residents from the home. Kyle shrugged his shoulders and

with his head down he kicked at a pebble on the path then turned away.

'You could have invited him to join us,' Alice said and looked up at Ellie. 'I wouldn't mind, and it looks like he needs cheering up a bit?'

Ellie snorted and pushed the wheelchair up to the table. 'I'll get you a cup of tea,' she said and put the brake back on to secure its position.

Her hand was close to Alice's, and she took hold of it. 'Forget the tea, you didn't answer my question? What's happened between you two?'

She watched Ellie bite her lip then sigh. 'Well, we had a big bust up at the weekend.'

Alice sighed. 'Ah, I see.'

Ellie's voice wobbled when she said. 'Kyle's parents are quite posh and have made it obvious they'd rather him marry someone in a professional career. So…'

Alice squeezed Ellie's hand which was now trembling. 'And what did Kyle say?'

'Well, Kyle told them he wasn't bothered what I did,' she said and gave a small sob. 'And that he loved me the way I was.'

Alice knew living up to the in-laws wouldn't be easy and made a quick decision. 'Well, that's good, right?' She said, 'And do you still love him?'

Ellie rested her head of copper curls on Alice's shoulder. 'Of course, I do!' She cried. 'But they're never going to accept me and all I can see ahead is upset and trouble, especially for Kyle. Which is what I told him at the weekend.'

Alice stroked the top of Ellie's head. 'Well, I can tell you love him because you're putting him and his feelings before your own, which is exactly what I did with Jim.'

Ellie lifted her head. 'S…so, did it happen to you, too?'

Alice nodded and looked into Ellie's big tearful eyes. 'My Jim was a bus driver when I first met him, but I knew he was destined for bigger things. My father wanted me to marry a man who was the son of his friend. He was training to be a doctor at the time, but I refused.'

Handing Ellie, a tissue from her bag, Alice watched her blow her nose and dry her wet eyes.

'Really,' Ellie said.

Alice nodded. 'The trainee doctor married a law student, and I married my Jim who eventually became a transport manager for a major firm. He was very well thought of within the transport sector with a much better salary than what a doctor could make, and we had a cracking good pension. But even without the money I couldn't have chosen a better man. Jim's love was worth a hundred doctors and my father had to admit that he'd been wrong.'

Ellie nodded and lifted her chin. 'Okay, so I'll get us both a cup of tea,' she said. 'And we'll start with a piece of Battenburg cake.'

Alice smiled. 'That'll be lovely but I'd much rather you go after Kyle first before he disappears.'

She could see Ellie wavering. It was as though the young girl's mind was working overtime when she said, 'Well, although I love my job at the nursing home, Alice, I suppose I could go on to do other things, like your Jim did?'

Alice had a lump in her throat when Ellie said her husband's name. She knew she'd gotten through to her, and croaked, 'Yes, of course! You can do anything, Ellie, once you've set your mind to it. I've watched you over the last year. You're bright, professional, caring, and loyal to the home and that counts for a lot in an employer's mindset.'

'Yeah,' Ellie muttered more to herself. 'I could be a team leader or even a floor supervisor if I tried hard.'

Alice grinned. 'Or even the manager of the home,' she said, 'but heck, why stop there? In ten years' time you could be running a whole group of nursing homes!'

Ellie giggled and gently pushed her shoulder. 'Oh, give over, Alice, you're just trying to make me feel better now.'

And it had worked, thought Alice. She had tried to boost the girl's confidence which in turn might make her realise that she was as good as anyone else to marry Kyle.

Ellie stared across the tables to where he was leaning against a lamp post chatting to another man.

Alice followed her gaze. 'Poor, Kyle,' she said. 'It looks as if his life has crashed down around his ears.'

'Well, I don't know if he'll still be interested after I've ignored him all weekend,' Ellie said. 'And I was a bit rude and huffy with him before.'

'Oh, I think he'll be more than interested, Ellie. My Jim used to look at me like that. It made me feel special as if I were the only girl in the world. It was as if he could see right inside me.'

Ellie swayed slightly from one foot to another. 'You think so?'

'I know so,' Alice said. 'I can see the love shining in his eyes when he looks at you. And I know it's different nowadays, but some things don't change,' she said then put her hand in the small of Ellie's back giving her a gentle shove. 'Go on,' she said. 'If he's the right one, go and get him.'

Ellie moved forwards. 'But your tea? And I'm not supposed to leave you?'

Alice shook her head. 'The other carers are just opposite, and the breaks are on this confounded wheelchair so I'm not going anywhere. Now, get across there or you might spend the rest of your life regretting it!'

Ellie practically flew around the tables to Kyle and Alice grinned. The young girl must feel as if there's no one else in the world but them two because that's how she'd felt with Jim. Alice could see the same special oneness as a couple that they'd shared and although she had lost Jim aged eighty, it had been the same until the day he passed.

She saw Kyle pick Ellie up in the air and spin her around while her friend squealed with joy.

Alice smiled then muttered to herself, 'And life's too short for regrets, Ellie.'

.....

And They Sang 'Shang-A-Lang'

Maureen Taylor

Your teenage years are hard to live through.
So many choices, and what did you do?

Did you send your spirit skyward with Norman Greenbaum,
or lace up your DM's for Slade's crazeee stomp down?

Did you glitter and glam with your Bolan perm,
or sway in your paisley smock to Procol Harum?

Did you join the blood and mayhem in Alice Cooper's school,
or cry into your ankle socks when Donny's love was cruel?

But now that you are 64, with your valentine,
Birthday greetings, and bottle of wine,

You still like a granny bop to the Shang-a- Lang sound,
And can't help pointing madly to that silver lined cloud.

But I bet you won't admit it, just to prove that you're still spry,
There's nothing like a little bit of Gangnam Style with Psy.

.....

A Lifetime in Footsteps

Shirley Fall

As a child Rosie loved plodging on the edge of the river - loved the feeling of the mud squelching in between her toes and hearing the sound of oozing as she pulled each of her small feet from the sucking surface. You couldn't stay still for long her brother, two years her senior, had warned, otherwise it might suck you down deep. These tidal mudflats were dangerous playgrounds for small children, and there were
no grown-ups around to call out advice, to warn of going in too deeply. Rosie smiled as she hauled her left foot out with a glorious guzzling sound that ended with a pop. She laughed in satisfaction as she clambered back onto the wooden staithes to safety, her slimy foot slipping slightly. What a fabulous way to spend a late autumn day, bathed in warm sunshine even though her feet were a little chilly. They would soon warm.

Somewhat later Rosie looked out of the window and knew what she should do. She was a bright young teenager with a sense of adventure and the outside was beckoning her to join it. She donned a woolly bobble hat and scarf and pulled on her cosy mitts. Her feet sank into her comfy boots just before she departed the warmth of the hallway. Almost immediately she was covered by a flurry of white flakes which rested on her eyelashes and tickled her nose. Setting off across the lawn towards the woods Rosie kicked her way through six inches of snow leaving a track to show which way she had come. In front of her the virgin covering of white was hers alone to conquer. How she loved this sense of being the first to

leave her mark, to make decisions that others could follow, to leave routes that others might pursue. Should she make a snow angel or launch herself into that drift where the snow had blown deep - so many choices presented themselves, all for her to decide upon. Years later Rosie walked along the grassy terrace above the Lakeland valley renowned for its daffodils, immortalised in poetry. She loved the fellsides and the freedom that they afforded the lone walker. She was well prepared and could stay out all day - self-sufficiency was her motto and Rosie lived up to it. Her boots left little sign of their passing as the path became rocky although her footsteps crunched satisfyingly as she made her way forward. Warm springtime sunshine caressed her shoulders and the smell of sap rising in the newly-leafed trees made Rosie smile. It was great to be free to do as you will in such a lovely landscape.

Now as Rosie stepped out onto the yellow sands, still warm underfoot, she all but fell and reached out for Stu's hand. It was safe and secure. "Steady there, girl - no mishaps," he reassured her. Rosie didn't want to tumble as had happened to so many of her friends - she was glad of the reassuring grasp. So much had changed in the recent years, things that Rosie would never have foretold or believed. She had had a whirlwind romance on one of her lone adventures and now there were two sets of footsteps to follow as they stepped onto the soft wet sand. Two sets of prints that came together at the water's edge as Rosie and Stu watched the sun sink below the western horizon.

Rosie smiled in contented satisfaction, as she reflected on a life well-walked.

.....

One Sultry Day

Anita Langham

Spare a thought for this single dad,
I'm doing my best, I'm a lonely lad.
It's all the fault of the sultry day
A certain hen-party came my way

I couldn't resist it, I took a chance,
I rocked right up, I began to dance.
That day I met the love of my life
As I thought then, my future wife.

Seemed she liked my moves, so then
I shook my booty, but it was when
I spoke to her in my baritone voice
I saw at once she'd made her choice.

I believed I'd found the perfect fit,
I was carried away I have to admit,
Things progressed in the usual fashion,
Followed by nights of torrid passion.

But I was accused, to my utter dismay
Of getting them *all* in the family way.
As time went by, they all grew moody
Then to my amazement, I grew broody.

Once they gave birth, they tittled off,
The love of my life was heard to scoff
You got us into this scrape, you git,
You made your bed, you can lie on it.

Us girls are ready for our next fling,
It's down to you - do the decent thing!
So, I'm rearing the kids all on my own,
They're happy, thriving and well-grown.

When I say I'm run ragged night and day,
'Tough! You had it coming', the mothers say.
'The arrogance of your pathetic prancing,
Your booming voice, your dirty dancing!

You macho rheas don't get it alas,
Girls rule the roost on Las Pampas!'

.....

1976

Valentina Short

The summer of 1976 was hot.

The heat was energy sapping and even the flies buzzed languidly. Everything looked bright, the sky, completely blue, held no breeze, no let up. Even in the shade it was over 80 degrees Fahrenheit. Roads melted, the elderly died and only the foolish ventured out at midday. A hosepipe ban was to last for some time, we heard, but the summer holidays were about to begin and my sister and I didn't give two hoots about any hosepipe ban. We were going to get tanned this summer.

Little did we realise that more than just the weather would heat up that year.

Marie was four years older than me, dripping with cool in the way only a 16-year-old blonde teenager could. And even though she was a hit with the boys she was also a no-nonsense 'don't mess with me' kind of gal.

Back then, our mother, known by some of the less worldly locals as a 'half-caste', because her mother was black and her father white, lived in the days before political correctness and the European Union. Although British, she'd been told to go home more than once due to her mocha skin and dark brown hair. She and her large family had already been kicked out of India when British rule ended in the 1950's. Her escape from the slum maisonette in Birmingham where they'd found themselves living secured only by training to be a nurse. Once qualified she moved to the northeast of England. There, she'd met our father. You could say they were literally black and white, like pieces on a chess board, but their differences went further than skin colour. He was a born and bred North East man – a true 'Geordie'. He worked in the shipyards and at least four evenings a week after work washed the dirt off, spruced up and went to the local Boiler Maker's Working Men's Club. Women were by invite only, and he didn't invite my mother often. If he wasn't there he was in the garden or fixing our battered Vauxhall Viva. Our mother, a Townswomen's Guild member, liked to let people know that she'd lived abroad until she was 17, she'd come from money, knew how to speak the Queen's English and could set a table for silver service, she'd even had a Governess.

But our parents did have a couple of things in common. They both believed they were better than any of our neighbours, and they both had affairs. He with a shoe shop assistant. She with a hospital porter. Very sophisticated.

That year, as my sister and I headed outside to get our tans, she was planning her escape from our home, and I was planning how I would survive her departure. Unbeknown to us other things were about to rock our world too.

The heatwave was in full force, burning through the country at 86 degrees Fahrenheit. But it was probably hotter on our improvised sun deck – a garage base, where we lay surrounded by the other council houses on the estate and the allotment that our father called the 'garden'. The garage base – a concrete slab had been laid single handedly by our father. It was a thing of pride for him. There was no garage yet, but the base for it lay three by six yards, big enough for deck chairs and beach towels.

We looked every part the coolest girls in town. My sister in her blue halter-neck dress and me in my silver hot-pants. It might have been a heatwave but we were sub-zero cool. After sitting in the deckchairs for a while we got down to the business of serious sun-tanning. Peeled down to our bathers and smearing ourselves with olive oil, we laid our towels out and ourselves down on the cement. We were determined to be brown by 5pm. The summer holidays were just beginning and even the lure of school holiday TV couldn't keep us from that cement base.

The radio next to us bleated out Elton and Kiki and as Thin Lizzy told us that the boys were back in town I drifted off, the ripples in the cement near my face just a blur, as I imagined my body as brown as Shirley Bassey's. We lay there more or less all day, listening to the radio, reading 'The Jackie' and talking about vitally important things such as how to not get caught smoking tabs. But, in terms of a tan, all I got, all *we* got, were bad cases of sunburn and freckles that threatened to join up into embarrassing blobs of brown.

That summer, that heatwave. It held so much promise and as we lay there in our posh cooking oil we were convinced that we were okay.

It wasn't long after that idyllic day that the inevitable split happened between our parents. Our father left for the shoe shop assistant and our mother took to sobbing in the bathroom or burning photos of our father. At one point she made a voodoo doll of him. We were never certain if it had worked, but years later when I saw him again he'd been struck by Bell's palsy.

The evening of the big split I remember my skin blistering like pork crackling after another day's successful tanning. As we headed in for tea, we could tell that our mother was in one of her moods. Sure enough, our father got home from work and we watched as the evening performance began. Fridays were usually the worst and we had front row seats.

As we sat around the kitchen table, the washing machine rumbled away in the background like thunder, as if it knew there would soon be sparks of lightning.

Our mother made the first move by slamming the food onto the plate. "I suppose you're going out again tonight. Is it the club or are you seeing *that woman*, the slut from the shoe shop?"

It was at points such as these that it was safest for me and my sister to look sharp and evacuate from the kitchen without making eye contact with either parent, leaving them to fight it out. We knew this particular fight wouldn't last long because it was Friday and our father had things other than our mother set in his sights. He only had a certain amount of time to get bathed, spruced up and hair combed back, for his 7pm rendezvous with *that woman*.

We knew this because my sister had seen them together on more than one occasion when she was out with her mates having a sly ciggy in the local woods, and he was with 'that woman', no doubt having a sly shag in the back of the Vauxhall Viva. It was all happening in the local woods, just three miles down the road from our house.

But there was something different about tonight's scrap. The name calling and insults reached a crescendo at about 6.30pm, slower than usual. Dad called my sister a slut for going into the woods with boys, but really it was because he knew she'd seen him in the car with the other woman. Then my mother called him a bastard for having carnal relations in the family car with 'that whore' from the shoe shop.

Suddenly our father emerged from the kitchen, face as red as if he'd been sunbathing on the garage base with us, but it wasn't because of what our mother had said to him. Our mother followed, still screaming, but this time she had the bread knife in her hand. "I'd rather kill you than see you with that whore again". Things were really heating up, but as she lunged at him my father grabbed the knife like David Carradine out of Kung Fu, cutting his palm in the process.

"You black bitch – that's it – I'm gone now and I won't be back"

With that he stormed out of the house, without his bath and with a tea towel wrapped around his bloody hand.

We didn't see him again for a fortnight, and when we did it was only long enough for him to pack his bags.

Our mother, an emotional wreck by now, sobbed and pleaded with him as he calmly found a suitcase and began to pack it. She begged him to return, but it was as pointless as giving the Devil hot coals.

Soon enough, the heat of summer ended as did the hosepipe ban. Our mother, my sister and I all felt the cold of autumn heading our way.

By the following summer our dad was living with his shoe shop assistant. Our mother had found her feet again with an insurance salesman and was disco dancing every week at the local discotheque, no doubt to Donna Summer who was also feeling love.

My sister, 17 by then, was off to be a cadet nurse and as for me…

I'd found the way to survive my sister's departure. It was punk and it was going to be my escape until I too was old enough to find my own freedom. 1977 didn't deliver on the heat of its predecessor, but as I lay there on the cement base that never got turned into a garage, listening to the Sex Pistols, and the Stranglers I pondered whatever happened to the Heroes and knew that sometimes, the best thing to be in life was Pretty Vacant.

.....

Five Days of Summer

Pat Atkinson

Summer speaks to me of music festivals. Such fun where teens, tweens, twenties and more can experience something magical. A time to forget work stresses and cost of living rises. Dress down, follow the crowds, pitch a tent, attach something distinctive to the dome, you will never find it again amid a myriad similar igloo shaped blue canvas tents. Trudge the long grass, trudge the squelchy grass, lose your wellies in the mud, still having fun. Music blasting out, swaying, dancing, waving, clapping, hooting, having a blast. Oh yes! I lose myself for five days every summer. Long live Glastonbury.

Come Monday I will be smartly attired, respectable, confident, conscientious, ready to deal with any problem that comes my way, and I will remember brilliant singers and musicians, being in a crowd moving as one. There is no upper age limit for revellers nor, it seems, performers. Rock on Tom, Paul and Diana.

.....

One Summer

Maureen Taylor

'Glad you're joining us, Tony. We usually start the session with a bit of wild writing,' said the teacher, 'I'm asking you all to write for five minutes, without stopping, about an unusual event, a strange coincidence, or even an encounter with a ghost. It might be something someone has told us about, or something we have experienced ourselves. Is that OK, everyone?'

Tony was keen to join the creative writing class but he was nervous on the first evening, of course. He tried to collect his thoughts for the exercise. He didn't expect to be plunged in at the deep end like this. Above the sound of hands moving across the pages as everyone started writing, Tony could hear a blackbird's shrill chirrup coming from outside. Staring at the blank page in front of him, his vision began to blur. Lifting his head to adjust his eyes, his view of the classroom became obscured by bright lights and coloured stars floating across his line of sight. He heard distorted voices echoing incoherently inside his head. He rubbed his eyes and his ears very hard to try to regain some clarity.

Looking down, instead of the grubby, grey carpet of the classroom, Tony saw meadow grass beneath his feet, very small feet, wearing sandals. He flexed his shoulders as the warmth of a summer sun pervaded his body. The blackbird he first heard was joined by numerous other birds singing and calling. He breathed deeply, and he could smell scents of the open air, gorse, oilseed rape. His attention was caught by a distant, half familiar voice calling his name. He turned to see his mother, her much younger self, kneeling on a picnic blanket in the shade of a tree. She was wearing the wide brimmed sun hat that she always wore in the summer.

'Don't go too far, Tony, darling.' he could hear her say. 'I'll get the lunch ready and I'll give you a call when you need to come.'

Tony squinted in the bright sunshine and set off down the hill. When he saw the old ruin at the end of the field, he knew he was back in his childhood home. Brushing the tops of the long grass with the palm of his hand, Tony walked slowly towards the stream he knew he would find at the foot of the hill. He thought he could see something moving in the heat haze and he stopped to gaze into the gap between the trees. Through half closed eyes, he could see two figures gradually emerge into full view, a man and a boy. At first, he thought he was seeing a shooter, with a rifle over the crook of his arm. But, instead of hunters' greens and boots, the man was wearing a loose shirt over breeches. What he thought was a rifle was just a pointed staff, and, when something glinted in the sun, Tony saw a dagger hanging from the man's belt. On seeing Tony, the man put his arm around the shoulders of the boy and drew him close. The boy was about the same age as Tony, but he didn't recognise him from the village or from school.

The man looked around the open space and called to Tony,

'Hey, laddie, which way north?'

Tony knew the compass points and indicated. The man raised his hand in thanks and ushered the boy in the direction he had shown them. Tony raised his hand in response, and he watched them until they were again consumed in the haze of the heat.

Hearing his mother call, Tony raced back up the rise and flopped down on the picnic blanket.

'What were you looking at? It must have been something very interesting?' she asked. 'You didn't hear me when I was calling.'

'Just a boy and his dad, but they weren't from around here. They looked a bit scruffy, really. They've gone now.'

'Mmm', says his mother, 'They must be from the caravan park. What do you suppose they were doing here?'

'Don't know,' Tony shrugged. 'Maybe just having a look around. Or maybe they were after rabbits. The man had a dagger. What shall we do after lunch?'

'Tony, I think it is going to rain, after all,' said his mother. 'I think we should pack up and go back home.'

Tony knew it wasn't going to rain, but he didn't argue. He wanted to go to Patrick's house because his mother always gave them chocolate biscuits and let them watch videos, even on a summer afternoon. As she quickly wrapped up the picnic in the blanket, Tony's mother asked him more questions about the man he had seen, but Tony preferred to chat about other more important matters, such as his cricket match on Saturday. It was the summer, he was ten years old and there were so many other things to capture his interest.

'Right, everyone. Time's up,'

On hearing the teacher's voice, Tony opened his eyes and found himself jolted back into the classroom. In contrast to the summer sunshine he had left behind, the artificial light cast a shadowy gloom, and it was dark outside. He screwed up his eyes and shook his head to re-focus. Looking down, he saw the blank page in front of him.

'Who would like to start us off?' said the teacher, 'Tony, you seemed to be deep in thought. Have you got anything you would like to share?'

'I'm really sorry,' said Tony. 'I just couldn't think of anything to write about.'

.....

Black Dog

Alwyn Bathan

It was probably not a good idea to sample so many drinks in one go, I told myself.

I was altogether too hot. The lapping of the waves and the sea breeze were not helping at all. As I pulled myself to sit, beads of sweat rolled down my brow. My stomach lurched.

That was definitely a result of the raspberry gin.

I glanced round, checking I hadn't been seen. There was no-one on the sand but me. I drew the carrier bag with my sandals nearer. Just in case. My brain's craving for flavoured gins was not reciprocated by the rest of my body.

Shedding layers was the next thing to do. I looked down. I was wearing a cardigan…in this heat? I tried to recall the night before, the shenanigans that resulted in choosing the beach as my non-human companion again. But, no memory was strong enough to puncture through the alcohol-induced fog. My stomach churned. It was time to divest before that carrier bag might need to be repurposed as my onshore sickbag. I checked to make sure no-one was watching. Any onlookers would be tutting at the sight. They usually did.

My buttons were putting up more of a fight than expected. Either that, or my hands were shaking more than usual. After the successful release of the first button, I stared out to sea to clear my mind. I wanted to focus on the horizon and the task in hand. To my left, I heard the panting of a dog bounding towards me, its racing paws scuffing across the hard surface like a thoroughbred, and I turned to the sound, to find myself face-to-face with the dripping nose of a large black creature.

I love dogs. I narrowed my tired eyes, tried to work out the breed. It was too tall and slim for a Staffie, longer-haired than a Rottweiler. And black, so absolutely black.

It was like no dog I'd ever seen before.

Through half closed eyes, I scoured along the beach. The piercing heat of the sun was attempting to laser-remove my corneas. I raised my hand to my brow, protecting my sight from its worst effects, but still couldn't see anyone.

My canine companion, panting hard, tongue lolling from his mouth, stared relentlessly at me, his dark eyes totally focused on my sweating face.

Did the creature think I was someone he knew?

His ebony coat was wet from the sea and frosted with grains of sand as he suddenly lurched towards me. I flinched, expecting the nip of his sharp teeth or the scratch of his claws.

As I opened my eyes to face him, there was no pain, but the pooch nuzzled forward and tugged determinedly on a button of my cardigan. He backed up, his sinewy hind legs digging into the yellow beach, until the garment was stretched taut between me and him. Maintaining my gaze, he reversed back...back...back as far as it would allow, before letting go. The knitting pinged once more into shape, but again, he approached to repeat his manoeuvre, his paws scraping into the dense foreshore.

Then, I realised what he wanted. For me to get up, pat him maybe, or throw a stick for him to fetch. Concentrating hard on maintaining my balance, I stood slowly, my feet planted firmly on the shore, looking out at the horizon. Falling over was never dignified.

Once upright, the black hound sat before me, his smiley mouth panting hard, his tongue lolling carelessly from his muzzle. His chest heaved but his body was still. He edged away, then stopped. His head tilted and he whined, his high notes chalking down the fragile blackboard inside my brain. He continued until I moved towards him. He repeated his game, edging me closer to the foam. My nerves jangled – I hate the movement of the sea. He'd lost a ball or a stick in the waves, I thought.

Where *was* his owner? I looked at him more closely. Although large and imposing, he was unkempt. His charcoal coat was dull and scruffy and his tail was still, but he persisted with his game, nudging me ever closer towards the water's edge.

'What is it, boy? Lost your ball?' I muttered, scanning the bubbles.

The movement of the waves lapping the shore made me feel unsteady. The inward, outward motion drew my gaze and played games with my balance. A brightly coloured ring or toy would surely be offered up by the spume to explain the mutt's behaviour. I worked hard to stay upright, my calf and thigh muscles tensing to avoid immersion into the foam. The sea reached my toes, as cold as iron on my skin. I focused again on the rolling bubbles as they swept towards me, then frivolously away, out to sea, with not a care in the world.

That simple cyclical movement just repeats.

No matter what's happening in your life.

Lose your money and the waves will continue.

Lose your job or your loved ones and the lapping will perpetuate.

It made me dizzy, and I could feel myself being drawn ever closer to that undesired baptism in the cold ebb and flow.

Suddenly with force, I was projected forward into the briny froth, my mouth and nose injected by a sting of icy saltwater. Battling to shake it away, I felt a heavy pressure in the hollow of my spine. Sharp claws stabbed at my skin, the full weight of the black creature holding me down under the waves. I scrabbled to shift its mass from me, struggling to breathe, to move and fight back, every muscle contracted and solid from the cold.

It took seconds I guess, a little more maybe, but felt like an infinity.

Clawing and scraping my way from the water, I flopped like an abandoned starfish onto the cool sand and prayed for the mid-day sun to warm my blue-veined flesh. My heart pounded and lungs screamed for air as I rolled open-mouthed, like some carelessly abandoned guppy-the prize no-one wants from the fayre. I turned my head to look along the beach. There must be someone to help. Somebody in control of this mad critter.

But, I was still alone on the deserted shore.

Just me, and that raven-haired mutt, my sole companion.

He caught my gaze as I peered at him, and bounded towards me, jumping with glee onto my chest, exploding away the remaining breath in my body. He pinned me to the beach, his front paws planted full square on my rib cage in an expression of mongrel victory. Salty droplets fell from his coat and landed on my face, making my eyes smart.

At last, I heard footsteps coming from behind the creature. They became louder, scuffing rhythmically across the hard shoreline.

Someone, at last.

I allowed a sigh of relief to depart my lungs. Above me, the cur stared fixedly on the person approaching. The animal was still, except for his tongue which dangled limply over my face, dispensing droplets of his saliva onto my wet skin.

The advancing footsteps must be his owner, I thought.

His ink-black tail started to wag, flicking sandy grains around him in a shower of salty hail.

I blinked and screwed up my eyes. The sun didn't help. I needed to clear my vision, set my gaze on this careless individual. I tried to turn to the owner, to give them a piece of my mind. This beast was too strong, too powerful to unleash on the unprepared, the vulnerable, those unable to defend themselves.

I struggled to breathe, the animal's weight still pressing down, stopping me calling to his master, to get him under control, let me get up and be on my way once more.

Outlined in the searing sun, a figure in dark clothing loomed into my peripheral vision. He approached slowly and, without words, laid down a long object. He stooped over me, a hood shadowing his face from the sun. I squinted to see him more clearly.

'Thank God you're here,' I whispered, still unable to speak with any volume. '*That dog* is out of control.'

He seemed not to hear, and there was a long silence, punctuated only by the hound's panting.

'Apologies,' he began. 'He thought you were…ready.'

'*He* thought?....Ready….*ready for what*?' I wanted to know.

'He seldom makes mistakes,' drawled the gravelly voice. But then, his tone changed as he addressed the creature directly. 'Black dog, it is not yet time for *this* one. The substances will hasten our mission, but we shall wait until there is no fight remaining. Until then, we have work elsewhere.' He clicked his fingers in the dog's direction and picked up the wooden staff he'd placed on the beach. He turned and walked away in the opposite direction.

With his master's words, the black beast bounded off alongside his keeper, leaving me breathless and exhausted in the glistening sand.

.....

AUTUMN

trees shed their coats

for a second-hand carpet.

tiny feet will play

Caroline Davison

Autumn in the Highlands

Valentina Short

Autumns in the Highlands were like nowhere else as far as we were concerned. At home there was a sense of life starting to shut down for winter as trees dropped their leaves and began to curl into themselves in preparation for the coming cold. But here in the Highlands of Scotland it felt as if the mountains, the sky, the animals were just awakening, returning to life after the fierceness of summer. The mountains with their browns, purples and greens seemed to pulsate as the wind rushed through them, arousing the stags, antlers proud and bodies pumping with hormones that spurred them into rutting and fighting for their hinds. The skies, showing the true scale of autumn here, punctuated with clouds that rolled by quickly, while the water in the mountain streams tasted crisper and fresher, as if ice had been added to their veins.

It was this magical and enchanted place that cemented our love of the Highlands in autumn. After walking amongst the heather and bog for an hour we finally reached the foot of the mountain – Buachaille Etive Mor or The Great Herdsman of Etive. A proper looking mountain – pointed apex and shrouded in mist at the summit. We were going up it to get engaged, and afterwards it would forever be 'our mountain', in this fairy-tale place where the autumn weather put paid to the vicious Scottish midges and the whisky always flowed in our hotel bar.

We came to know that hotel, its bar and its staff very well over the years, returning each autumn as if magnetically pulled north by invisible threads that wove through all the mountains and streams in the Highlands. It had been built in the 1700s – an old drovers stop. Used by the King's soldiers when their slaughter of the MacDonalds was carried out. Now a warm and inviting, albeit dilapidated hotel, it suited us perfectly. Probably last decorated in the 1970s, it was warm and lovely, filled with mountaineering paraphernalia and photos of long-gone mountaineering heroes. The hotel and bar staff seemed as hypnotically drawn to the hotel as we were, and their familiar faces greeted us each time we returned.

That was where we met Angus - born and bred five miles up the road in a tiny village called Ballachulish. Angus had expanded his world just enough to go to university in Aberdeen before returning to the Highlands to secure a job behind the bar of the hotel. His Scottish accent and Scottish attitude always assured us of a lively conversation. He knew every inch of the Highlands having been up most of the mountains and in most of the lochs. Angus always had a good tale for us Sassenachs. We thought he'd always be there, year after year, when we returned. He was part of our magic, but now after working in the hotel for five years Angus was getting ready to broaden his world further.

We travelled up on a Friday and didn't see Angus until the next day. When we did, he was sitting on the wrong side of the bar. He was on our side. He told us he was off to Glasgow the next day to catch a plane to Australia. He had been saving and now had enough cash to 'move-on'. He was going to learn how to surf and then teach others.

"Let us buy you a drink, Angus", said my husband. "I'll miss you Angus," I said.

Angus gladly took the drink, in fact he took several, and by early afternoon we all agreed we'd be better continuing our conversation outside in front of the hotel, in the crisp autumn air. It was glorious out there, and for once in the Highlands clear blue skies boasted right in front of us. And there, less than a mile away from us, as if to send us completely giddy was our mountain.

Hotel guests arrived and disappeared inside, and eventually the light began to fade. Angus by now was exceedingly drunk. When we decided to order food, we thought it prudent to buy Angus some too, as he told us with great mirth that he hadn't eaten all day and had no cash. "All tied up in the Australian adventure", he slurred. The three of us ate and drank some more until our mountain was just a dark shape against dark skies.

Eventually Angus said his thanks and farewells. We hugged and wished him well as we watched him stagger towards the staff quarters. I believe I may even have shed a tear for him. It reminded us of watching our own son head off to university.

And that was that. The next day we awoke with sore heads and looking at our watches knew Angus would be on his way to Glasgow Airport with his own hangover. We were glad we'd fed him at least.

After a few more days our holiday was over. As we headed back down the road to England passing moors and lochs, we got the sense that there was a change in the air around our beautiful mountain. We wondered what else might be different by the time of our next return.

We spent the year at work, meeting up with family, friends, doing the things we usually did all year round, but as spring and summer passed, we knew it would soon be time to pack our bags and the car and head back up the road to the place where we felt we could truly breathe.

We drove past Loch Lomond in the Trossachs and then finally beyond Tyndrum. Up and on into the Highlands we went, through the snow gates which always held a fascination for us, as we wondered how often they got closed. Speaking out loud we said the familiar place names that we loved so much – Firkin Point, Crianlarich, Bridge of Orchy.

Eventually we arrived at the hotel, marvelling again at just how beautiful this place was in autumn. This was year seven for us. As we reached the hotel we were pleased to see the usual guys hanging around outside. The biggest one had fourteen point antlers, while his harem of about 15 hinds nibbled the hotel grass contentedly. Many people came by just to see the deer at the Hotel, and today was no exception. However, we were no newcomers and had a certain swagger to our step as we went past the deer through into the hotel reception area. Sure enough, the same old faces were there. Bess and Christine who came around from behind the desk to hug us and Bruce who shouted a cheery 'hello' as he carried wood through to the hotel lounge for the huge open fire.

By 7pm it was dark in the Highlands, but that didn't bother us. We hurried up to our room and throwing the window open hung our heads outside to breathe in the intoxicating air. Staring into the darkness, we could feel the autumn rain on our faces while listening to the mad and strained cries of the rutting stags, who we could only hear in the pitch black.

But, as we'd suspected the previous year, things were starting to change. The next morning, we missed the hotel owner. Her usual feisty presence at the breakfast tables, along with her massive Newfoundland dog was nowhere to be seen.

"Where's Betty?" we asked the staff. Bess told us that Betty had given the hotel to her son, and that she was enjoying some well-earned rest in her cottage nearby.

To us, Betty was just one more of the central characters who made that hotel *our* hotel, and the surrounding mountains and glens our special place.

We had our annual celebration up the mountain and enjoyed our time in Glencoe as we had done now for several years, but on the way home there was a silence in the car. Neither of us could voice what it was that was concerning us, but I guess we both knew that something was definitely changing in our place in the mountains.

It was by accident that we found out later that year that Betty's son had sold the hotel. A huge corporation had moved in, and the estate owner was glad to be working with them to build a new 'state of the art' hotel in the Highlands. Devastated, we watched from a distance via the world-wide-web to see what was happening to our hotel. We felt that if the hotel was to be radically altered, or worse still demolished, that our charmed autumns would be no longer either.

Sure enough, within a couple of years the old hotel was replaced by a new one – it looked to us like an industrial warehouse. No warmth – no charm. No familiar faces, just posh menus and even posher prices that we couldn't afford. By now all we could do was watch from our English home, mourning the fact that we couldn't go back. It wouldn't be the same. We would never see our mountain in the autumn again from the panoramic hotel windows of old.

Years passed, and the longing just intensified. We had to return to Glencoe somehow. We had to see our mountain, and we had to be there in autumn.

We knew that there was another hotel further down the glen. "It won't be the same," my husband said. "It won't have the views," I thought. But we gave it a go and decided to travel back. We'd been to the bar of that hotel in previous years after walking, but we knew it didn't have the view of our mountain and we didn't know the staff. However, we booked, and on our arrival, and to our great pleasure we found Bess sitting behind the reception desk – she too had moved on from our old hotel and now worked here instead. That cheered us greatly. Later that evening as we sat outside we could still hear stags rutting. We could still feel the autumn wind on our faces, and we could hear the nearby stream announcing its presence to us.

"I'm here it said – and you are here. You are back".

.....

Art in Autumn

Pat Atkinson

Who doesn't like a walk in the woods in autumn? The sights and sounds of the environment, any or all of which will lift your spirit, be a tonic for the soul, a moment of joy.

And who isn't tempted by the satisfying crunch of fallen leaves, a remnant of childhood? I like to collect autumn's offerings for collage purposes.

Try this: identify a tree, take a bark rubbing, gather some related leaves. On returning home make a collage of your treasures. Go further if you wish and frame it or photocopy it to use as personalised writing or wrapping paper. Go even further, laminate it and you will have a place mat to delight you.

You will be surprised at the outcome and you didn't think you had an artistic bone in your body!

.....

Acorn

Cecilia Coulson

Anxiously, together, glancing at celestial heavens above

Clouds are seen, as canopies of oak trees sway in the breeze,

Orange, brown, yellow, golden curled leaves lie as a carpet of love,

Rustled noisily by small boots, shuffling as they please,

Nuts gathered by squirrels; a winter pantry full of fallen acorns.

.....

Window

Caroline Davison

The plaintive notes of Simon and Garfunkel's song float across the room.
The leaves that are green certainly are turning to brown. Cracked and broken.
Like my heart.
Oh, don't be so dramatic! So, you misjudged the situation, so what?
So, if I had a violin, I'd shoot myself, mafia style, in a hail of bullets and spaghetti.
As it is, there is nothing romantic about a red eyed, squawking female wearing yesterday's t-shirt and outsized jogging pants.
My attire is a protest. Proof that I can do sloppy.
Oh, but what if the object of my devotions were to return right now?
Fat chance.
The swinging hangers tell their own story. I try not to relive the conversation that shattered my happiness, but the criticisms worm their way into my conscious thoughts.
Borderline cruel.
My flat is 'too neat', my clothing 'staid', and my choice of literature induces sleep, not excitement. Perhaps the most unforgivable comment was reserved for my cat, Edgar. *Edgar Rocket of Beadnell.* A handsome feline the size of a small dog with an attitude to match, who had shown his antipathy towards

my flatmate from the first nano second of their meeting. My precious Eddie was referred to as 'spiteful and vicious' with a desire to inflict pain wherever he could.

Ooh, that sounds familiar.

How could I have fallen for the charm offensive? Me. The great Counsellor. Happy to dispense wisdom to all who would stand still long enough.

Hah. It looks so easy in the textbooks. Endless lectures about 'attachment, cognitions, and delusions.' Well, perhaps it's time for a cognitive reappraisal.

Suddenly Edgar hurdles across the furniture and jumps onto the windowsill. His head turns from left to right as he watches the falling leaves, fascinated at nature's autumn display. He begins taking languid swipes at the interlopers. I join him. The game seems to soothe us both. He looks like a kitten again. Innocent and curious. I sit by the window ignoring the fact the temperature is dropping. Edgar seems to sense my slight shudder and steps gently onto my knee, giving me a nudge and a kiss.

The warmth of his body and his obvious love give me a feeling of security. He cares not one jot about what I'm wearing, my hairstyle or my habits. If there is love, food and warmth his world is complete.

A knock at the door echoes.

He walks with me towards it, poised to attack.

 'Hey Eddie'

My next-door neighbour has a canvas bag in one hand and a bottle of wine in the other. Edgar relaxes. This is a human he likes, and his purring indicates the visit is a welcome addition to our day.

There is no need for words, we embrace, the wine is opened, the meal is prepared.

A jazz CD is chosen, and we slip into a comfortable conversation.

Slowly, I begin to shed the leaves that have clouded my vision and I see for the first time that behind the smile there is real affection, hesitating to reveal itself. The comfort blanket of genuine warmth.

I could be wearing an elephant's tutu and this person would not judge me.

As day gives way to dusk, I stand by the window again, Edgar by my side. He gives me a knowing look.

Tomorrow I will invite my neighbour out for a picnic in the nearby park. We will kick leaves together, run together and let nature take whichever course she chooses.

.....

Death of Autumn

Pauline Bennett

The trees were turning golden and bronze, a sure sign that Autumn had arrived….

Dan and his wife, Lynne, had bought the cottage in the height of summer; it had been framed by blowsy trees and the scarlet Virginia Creeper had clung precariously to the pointed gables of the almost fairytale house. They couldn't understand why it had been so cheap; elderly lady, living on her own with no car, was the reason provided by the estate agent and, as it was Lynne's childhood dream, they hadn't hesitated.

It wasn't completely isolated - more on the end of a tiny hamlet high up on the Moors and, although Lynne had no car once Dan had left for work, this was no hardship. She loved walking and the garden was to be her project and there was no better time than the present to get started.

The front garden had three stunning lilac trees and the autumn flowers under them were still in bloom so Lynne decided to make a start on the back garden. A sizable challenge, but she had marked it carefully on a plan drawn up last Sunday afternoon. First, she would walk the plot and note any hazards or potential problems on her plan. Pulling her padded gilet on top of her thick jumper and with wellies already donned, Lynne closed the kitchen door behind her and, plan in hand, she started to meander down the garden. The first part of the rather wild garden would make an ideal vegetable plot—plenty of large stones to remove but the soil was dark, rich loam - not like the clay of their last garden where the only things that flourished were the slugs! No doubt this soil would have its challenges but there was no hurry - this was to be their lifetime dream project.

The morning passed calmly as little notes were attached to the plan and then, as she reached the old stone wall marking the end of the garden, she gasped in amazement at the beauty of what lay before her. The garden was bounded by a gurgling beck, its rushing waters singing as they bounced across the rocks and lapped the little stone wall, but beyond that lay a woodland filled with such stunning flowers it was impossible to believe it hadn't been planted deliberately. Laying down the plan and pen on the warm stones of the boundary wall, Lynne paused to work out the best route across to the flower filled glade. They were definitely not wild flowers. She had to get over there, so by carefully clambering to the top of the wall and seeking out a soft landing area, Lynne did it. She jumped and, although the ground had looked soft on the hummock she had picked, the velvety grass overlaid a hard rock; her knee scraped on the rock, but she simply rubbed the spot and looked for the way through. The tall reeds showed a boggy area to her left and without a handy stick to see what lay beneath the surface, Lynne was forced to jump across a series of flattish rocks - almost like stepping stones to reach the little clearing. At this moment the sun came out and the glade was bathed in a golden light which only accentuated the flowers. And she was right - these were no simple wild flowers, but a variety of almost every autumn flower she had ever come across in the enthusiastic catalogues pushing their way through her letterbox: Marguerites, pink Dianthus, tall yellow Goldenrod, Cyclamens and frothy Cosmos - this was a little haven of riotous colour. But why? Who had scrambled across the stream to make this delightful garden? Was it a child's garden? It was almost childlike in its colours and now she looked carefully, it did resemble a heart shape with a large Canna Lily hiding something, a stone or maybe a pet's grave, in the centre. Treading carefully, she bent over to touch a rough stone and scraping away the moss that covered it, she could feel some roughly carved letters. But her soft nails weren't up to the job so she would have to return with the correct tools. As she stood, pushing her long hair out of her eyes, she felt the sun's warmth dissipate as a cloud wandered its way across the sky and a slight chill breeze began to sigh its way across the glade. 'Time to go back and get a cuppa before I carry on,' she thought to herself and turning back towards her own garden she felt her heart sink as she realised that jumping across had been easy, but getting back was a much more difficult proposition. Pausing to plan out a route across the now darkened and slightly melancholy sounding stream, she felt a presence and turned abruptly. But, no, this was silly. There was no one there. Her imagination was running away.

As she began to clamber across the rocks towards the water, she heard the sound, a whimpering sound, like a child hurt or too worried to call out. Balancing on the next flat rock she turned, and again there was nothing to be seen, although the flowers seemed less dazzling now the sun had disappeared. Moving warily towards the stream, she hesitated to see at what point she could make a leap for the wall, her wellies would be under water at some point but, no matter, they would dry out by the aga. Then, as she took the plunge and stepped down into the rushing water, the whimpering became a cry of pain. Twisting round, her welly slipped and she felt herself tumbling into the water, her arms flailing wildly for a handhold on the stone wall. Then the sickening thud of her head on the wall itself. As she began to lose consciousness, and slumped into the now dark water, the long shriek of childish banshee laughter was the last thing she heard...'

What if…?

Cecilia Coulson

What if …

It was raining, during an autumn night.
The sun hidden by clouds, a feeling of discontent, no joy, only lethargy.
People scurrying to find a place of warmth and serenity?
But what if …

It was snowing, during a winter night.
Happiness pervades; snuggled under duvets with friends transcending heights.
Tired from creating snowmen, sledging and victorious in snowball fights?
But what if …

It was foggy, during a spring night,
Clouds cloak the emerging buds of foliage and shrubbery,
The city's infrastructure shrouded in a depressing fine filigree of drudgery?
But what if …

It was a heatwave, during a summer night
Hot, no sleep, tossing, twisting, twitching, turning
Waiting for early morning, to feel a degree of yearning?
But what if …

Sunrise slowly emerges, to embark on a new morning, a new beginning and a new awakening?

WINTER

in the icy web

are patterns of illusion

lacemaker for you.

Caroline Davison

Cottage on the Hill

Susan Willis

Stephen drove as quickly as possible through the water-logged roads to Otley in Yorkshire. He was desperate to see his mum after the storm. She still lived in their old family home up on the hill above the town. It was a white stone cottage which stood out in the landscape surrounded by a forest of trees.

He grimaced remembering the sentence she often said in his response to moving, 'You'll take me out of here in my coffin!'

It wasn't a big cottage, just two small bedrooms, but it was where he and his sister had been raised. Mum had lived there sixty-one years and there was no shifting her. His father had died years ago and now his mum was eighty and alone. It was a constant worry to him and his wife, Beth who adored his mum too. Over the last few years, he'd pleaded and begged for her to sell up, but she flatly refused.

The storm had raged the day before and although he'd tried twice to drive from Ilkley to Otley the road had been flooded then impassable by a fallen tree. When he'd previously looked at the weather forecast, they'd wanted her to come and stay with them. But she'd adamantly shaken her head and reassured him she would be fine.

Stephen chewed the bottom of his moustache and turned right into the town. He redialled her number again from the hands-free but still there was no answer. He groaned and rubbed his eye which felt full of grit because he'd hardly slept.

The noise of the storm outside their bedroom window had been bad enough but the worry of his mum alone in the cottage had kept him awake tossing and turning. He'd gazed out of their bedroom window at the ravaged countryside with streaks of silver lightening speeding across the darkness of the sky and shuddered.

Did she have power? Had she found the candles? Was she shivering with cold in her bedroom? Had she fallen on the stairs in the dark? Or worse still, fallen carrying a candle and the cottage had burned down around her? Had any of the old trees outside come down and crashed through the windows?

His mind had spun with fear because he couldn't reach her. There'd been no answer on either her mobile or landline. Part of him had raged against what he saw as her stubbornness to live there in her old age and thought it selfish.

He knew and understood the memories of their family home but all the same, he fretted every day about her. Not that he wanted her to go into an old people's home because he didn't, but last year he'd spotted a small bungalow in Otley town for sale and had taken her the details. In her usual obstinate manner, she'd tutted and refused to even look at them then tossed them onto the fire.

Stephen turned onto the narrow winding road uphill which was more of a rough dirt track than a proper road. He slowed down to a minimum because he could feel the earth was soft and wet under the car and didn't want to get stuck.

Beth had put fresh milk and bread with a few other necessities into the boot of his car this morning before he'd set off. She had wanted to join him, but he'd refused because he didn't know what awaited him at the cottage which might alarm her.

When Beth had given him the bag, she'd said, 'Stephen, it's her life and if Mum wants to stay up there alone that's up to her. You can't force her to leave - these are her decisions to make but do tell her again that we want her with us. I've got the guest bedroom ready just in case.'

Stephen smiled thinking of Beth. She was missing the two boys who had gone off to university and knew Beth was looking for someone to fuss over. It's what she did best.

He sighed however, and knew Beth was right about Mum making her own decisions but that didn't make it any easier for him.

He turned up the steeper hillside now and breathed a small sigh of relief. The track looked clear and because he knew all the trees and landscape as though he was blindfolded, he was confident there were no fallen trees.

He'd watched the storm news on TV early that morning with last night's images of trees crashing onto cars and into

windows resulting in fatalities which had only fuelled his anxiety.

Stephen took a deep breath and tried to apply the logical side to his mind. In the past when he'd worried about her then arrived to see her waiting at the door and all was well, he'd chastised himself for fretting. But that wasn't following a storm, he thought. He could only hope and pray today would be the same.

However, as he neared the cottage she wasn't at the door. He chewed his moustache again and felt his stomach churn. Where was she? She had always been able to hear a car on the dirt track from any room in the house, so why not today?

Stephen turned off the ignition, took a deep breath to bolster himself for what lay ahead then hurried through the back door into the large kitchen. It was empty. His heart raced when he hurried through the lounge which was also empty. Then tearing to the bottom of the staircase to run up, his mouth dried, and he croaked, 'Mum? Where are you!'

Silence surrounded him and he choked back a sob in his throat. Dear God, where was she? Outside amongst the trees? On the bathroom floor?

But then his shoulders sank, and he felt near collapse when she tottered through the passage from the downstairs toilet.

'Oh, Mum!' He shouted and ran to her.

He wrapped her into his arms and sighed with relief. The fear left his body and his legs felt weak and shaky. He dropped down into his father's armchair by the side of the fireplace. He bent forward and put his head in his hands. 'I was so frightened that I'd find you had fallen o...or worse?'

He felt her hand patting the top of his head then running her fingers through his hair. It reminded him of when he was little and had the recurrent bad dream that he'd been lost amongst the trees and couldn't find his way home.

Stephen leaned into her and expected to find her soft ample waist where he'd often buried his head. Instead, he felt her thin craggy hip bones which brought him back to the here and now. He shook his head abruptly.

'I'll make some tea,' she said busying off into the kitchen. She called through to him, 'And thank Beth for the milk, she's so thoughtful because I had run out last night.'

Settled and sipping their hot tea, Stephen pulled a face. 'Urgh, there's sugar in this!'

'It's good for shock,' she muttered and handed him the biscuit barrel which was full of his favourite jammy dodgers and chocolate digestives. He grinned.

She said, 'Well, it was a horrible storm. Probably the worst I can remember up here unless my memory is playing tricks with me.'

Stephen licked the chocolate from his fingers and let her talk.

She looked past him and out of the window. 'The sky was black at just four in the afternoon as if it was the middle of the night. The TV crackled, and the screen was all white blotches, but it didn't go off.'

He nodded and sipped the hot tea.

'Then through the night the lightning cracked off the bedroom window,' she said. 'I suppose if the windows had been double glazed, I wouldn't have heard the claps of thunder which were deafening! And I did try to ring you, but the landline was off and of course there's very little mobile signal even on a good day.'

He saw her hand tremble when she lifted the teapot to pour more tea. Her eyes darted around the fireplace. 'And yesterday, I thought there was something lodged in the old chimney,' she said. 'Because the noise was so scary...' she shivered and pulled a fluffy cardigan around her shoulders.

Stephen had installed a log burner last year and always made sure she had a stack of chopped logs but now he noticed she'd only used the smaller ones. Maybe the others were too heavy to lift? He picked up a big log and chucked it into the burner.

He saw her nod in satisfaction and his heart squeezed. He couldn't remember his mum ever using the word scary before, let alone look frightened.

She looked old and shrivelled up somehow. Gone was her strong robust figure that she'd always had. He stared at

her thin wasted arms which had been strong and chubby. A memory flashed through his mind of baking day when he was little. With flushed red cheeks and her sleeves rolled up to her elbows she'd roll out pastry to make pies and pasties. He smiled - how those big arms could hold him in a hug that near took his breath away.

But now she was small and frail. He gulped hard. If his father were here, he would be saddened to see her infirmity, and like himself, would think she was suffering in the cottage alone. But what else could he do?

'Yes, it was a bad night,' she admitted.

He sighed. 'Well, there's more to come according to the forecast because of this global warming,' he said. 'We can expect more flooding in the rivers as the rain moves down the hills and moors today.'

He saw her eyes widen at the thought. 'Well, at least I'm not near a river.'

He nodded and dunked another biscuit into his tea. 'No, but it means I can't get up to you every day if the roads are flooded!'

She nodded and stared into the burner.

He tried again. 'Please come and stay with us at least until the storm threats ease off then I'll get a good night's sleep not worrying about you up here alone?'

She nodded and he sensed an air of defeat around her wrinkled face.

He watched her take in a deep breath. 'Okay,' she said. 'I'll come until the weekend and maybe when I'm there, you could look for a small flat or bungalow near you?'

He gasped and quickly nodded in agreement before she could change her mind.

She smiled at him. 'I think it's time to say goodbye to the old place.'

.....

A Day to Remember

Cecilia Coulson

On a dank, dreary Thursday morning, sleet falls as teenagers Mary and Teresa dawdle towards the local train station. Teresa, the more adventurous one between the two of them, draws caricatures of snow men in the sleet which has fallen on the windscreens of the parked cars. A look of tedium soon etches on both their faces. They know this route inside out, the prestigious high school on the other side of the city being their destination.

The carriage is empty apart from one man. He looks to be in his 70s. His friendly, weather beaten face, thin frame, short grey hair and immaculately trimmed beard ooze an aura of distinction. A brown overcoat, fastened with round, leather buttons, a crimson muffler entwined around his scrawny neck. He sports brown leather boots, which look as if they've seen many a cold winter. The elderly gentleman is well protected from the biting wind and flurries of snow.

Mary and Teresa avoid eye contact with the elderly man. They pass him, then flop down onto tatty cloth seats sitting opposite each other, with a small table in front of them. They always choose to sit in seats with a table, so they can finish any homework they haven't managed to complete the night before. Teresa has a bird's eye view of their travelling companion.

'I'm freezing,' complains Teresa. 'I blumin' well wish I'd put me gloves on'. She places her hands on the small lukewarm heater under the window, a feeling of warmth tingles through her fingers.

Mary isn't listening to her, she is more concerned about the elderly gentleman.

'Is he looking at us? What's he doing?' she asks Teresa anxiously, not daring to turn around in case he thinks she's being nebby.

'He's just staring out of the window. I presume watching the world go by. Don't worry, he looks so friendly,' states Teresa.

'You might think he's friendly,' retorts Mary, 'but I've just got this funny feeling that he's up to no good.'

They reach the end of the line, but it isn't the end of their journey. The two girls grudgingly walk towards the trolleybus stop, directly outside the station's exit. They still have another twenty minutes journey to endure. The sky is leaden. The wind is now blowing a hoolie, causing snowflakes to swirl around, with not a care in the world. Landing on their green duffle coats, they create a mosaic pattern, then melt into the woollen fabric. The white landscape of the Victorian buildings, in the old city, looks picturesque, but the motor vehicles have difficulty navigating, the now brown slush covering the roads. Men, women and children trudge along the snow covered pavements, gratefully reaching their destinations, escaping from the ever increasingly inclement weather.

'I'm not happy,' says Mary, being sensible as always. Tapping Teresa on the shoulder she points upwards. 'I don't like the look of those skies. It looks as if we could be in for a snow storm. If a trolleybus doesn't turn up in the next ten minutes, let's get the train back home. What do you think, Teresa?'

Teresa doesn't answer. She's staring into the distance, not paying any attention to Mary's concerns about the worsening conditions.

'Can you see him? He's over there. The guy on the train. He's walking up Grainger Street. I wonder where he's going? Seems strange an elderly man being out in this weather.'

So many questions are rolling off Teresa's tongue, but all go unanswered, because the number 36 electric trolley bus pulls up in front of them.

'Hop on quickly girls,' shouts the conductor. 'Let's hope we can get you to your school in one piece.'

Two other passengers are onboard. The women are nattering about spending their well-earned wages in the many clothes, shoe shops and tearooms of Northumberland Street. The snow continues to fall, every snowflake turning and twisting silently, each distinctive in its own design. The trolleybus ride would normally take them on a scenic route through the centre of the city, but not today.

Ding dong!! The trolleybus quietly pulls away, heading in the direction of Grainger Street, one of the oldest streets in the city. It is built on a slight incline, enabling citizens to travel from the train station to the heart of the cosmopolis, suburbs and beyond. The girls sit at the front of the trolleybus, with a perfect view of their journey. They pass the 13th century church called St. John the Baptist, then the well known department store Wenger's comes into view. Teresa spies their travelling companion from the train pushing open the front door of the department store. The trolleybus's windscreen wipers fight to keep pace, as large dense snowflakes fall, coating the vehicle, as if draped in a white fluffy blanket. Then everything stops. The lights go out. No power. No electricity. The snowstorm intensifies, much to everyone's dismay. Mary and Teresa look at each other, both with trepidation and concern etched on their faces.

'Ooooooh, I'm frightened. What's going to happen to us? Will we ever get to school?' cries Mary.

'Oh! stop being so silly Mary. I'm more worried about that car, see. Look, look. What's happening? What's it doing?' questions Teresa, a look of horror in her eyes. 'Oh no!!!' a gasp of fear emanates from her innermost depths. She can't believe what she's seeing. It's sliding down the hill now, sideways on. It's got no grip in the snow. 'See, see!! It's coming towards us. It's going to hit the front of the trolleybus ….it can't stop!!' she exclaims. 'Someone's going to get hurt'.

Sure enough, a black Vauxhall Victor horizontally slides down the hill. No control whatsoever. Increasing in speed it slithers closer and closer towards the front of the trolleybus. It summersaults twice, landing the right way up. The hefty trolleybus brings it to a complete stop. The sound of the two vehicles entwined in a mash of steel bellow, like a wounded bull. Everyone on the trolleybus is shaken, but nobody is hurt.

Within seconds of the car coming to a standstill two people emerge, crawling through a broken window. A man in his early 20s and a young teenager. The man carries a suitcase, but as he jumps from the car he catches the clasp on the mangled window frame. The suitcase opens, spilling its contents onto the deepening snow. Gold bracelets, bejewelled pendants, silver and gold wrist watches, men's chunky gold chains glisten on top of the snow, like gold and silver hundreds and thousands sparkling on top of a white iced birthday cake.

A shop alarm wails loudly, its constant voice blaring above the stillness of the nigh on empty streets. The pervading noise distracts Mary's and Teresa's travelling companions from the accident. So much is happening. A young policeman runs around the corner, slips and slides in the snow, heading towards the mangled car and trolleybus. He's out of breath, but manages to shout in short, loud outbursts.

'Catch them, catch them. They've just robbed the big jeweller's shop around the corner, Northern Goldsmiths.'

The copper spies the two villains plodding through the deep snow, up the hill, towards Grey's Monument. He turns in their direction and gives chase….as best he can. He knows these scoundrels, they're always up to no good.

An elderly man, with a determined stride walks towards the crash. He's dressed in a bright red tunic, bright red trousers, and sports brown leather boots, which look as if they've seen many a cold winter. He carries a hessian sack over his right shoulder.

'Hey! Mary.' exclaims Teresa, 'That's the guy that was on the train with us. He looks as if he's dressed as Santa Claus'. She rushes to an open window shouting, 'Mister, mister,' attracting the man's attention 'Are you Santa Claus?'

'Yep,' comes the reply. I've been working at Wengers for the past 2 weeks. It's my last day today. Saw the crash….everybody OK?' He stands for a few minutes to get his breath. Affirmative nods from the passengers put his mind at rest. 'I'll check to see if there's anybody else in the car. You never know. Then I'll come back.'

Santa Claus trudges through the snow towards the car and throws his hessian sack down, before peering through the car windows. Mary all the while is vigilantly watching Santa Claus's every move, but Teresa sits down exhausted with all the confusion. After a few minutes Teresa turns towards Mary.

'Mary, are we ever going to……' She stops mid sentence. Mary isn't there. Where is she? Teresa gazes down the length of the trolleybus. She's not on the lower deck, maybe she's gone to the upper deck. With nibble feet she climbs the stairs, but, no, she's nowhere to be seen. Perplexed, she descends to be greeted by two Newcastle Corporation Bus Inspectors jumping onto the platform at the back of the trolleybus. They've come to escort the stranded passengers to safety.

'Help me, please. I can't find my friend anywhere. She's wearing a green duffle coat, the same as mine. One minute she was here and then she wasn't? She's called Mary. Where the heck has she got to?' Teresa urgently asks the two inspectors.

One of the Inspectors points across the road to a young girl, in a green duffle coat, straddled across Santa Claus, as two policemen approach the comic scene. Mary had seen Santa Claus surreptitiously collect all the jewellery lying in the snow, then without haste put it into his hessian sack.

Another two exhausted police officers clamber on board the trolleybus.

'Hello, folks. Just to let you know what's going on. That young lass over there has saved the day.' They direct their gaze at Santa Claus, now in handcuffs and Mary, who's beaming from ear to ear. 'Santa Claus over there, or to give him his full name Paddy Carr is the patriarch of a notorious criminal family in the west end of Newcastle. The two scoundrels that robbed the jeweller's shop are called Jimmy and Tommy Carr, they're his grandkids. They're all in this robbery together. The youngsters were to perform the deed and then granddad was to pick up the loot, but they didn't expect such a snowstorm. Lucky that young lass was adventurous enough to outwit the old man'.

An exhausted Mary staggers onboard the trolleybus. Everybody greets her with joy, so pleased that she's OK. She's a hero.

Teresa looks at her, tears in her eyes, concern in her voice.

'You could have been hurt, or even killed, you silly so and so. I'm supposed to be the adventurous one, and you're supposed to be the sensible one.' Teresa wraps her arms around Mary, an outward sign of relief.

'Well, I did tell you, didn't I?' smiles Mary, 'I thought he was up to no good. And I've been proved right.'

.....

A Winter Haiku

Anita Langham

We drift apart as

Cattle do when grass grows sparse

And fresh fields beckon

.....

Winter's Window

Edward Cartner

'Talk to a counsellor,' Jean had said a month ago, 'tell them what your window shows you now. It might help you come to terms with all this.'

I had never been too keen on this trendy counselling business, had always seen it as an intrusion. Besides, my 'window' is really Alice's. It wasn't exclusively private, but it is where she took calm inspiration, and, besides, I have left her paint-pots and brushes there as a messy, living memorial.

Still, I owed Jean a lot. She had seen her sister and the Seasons through the worst days, so I might as well take a fresh look through the window; the view hadn't changed, only familiarity had made it invisible.

It was unbelievable that two years had passed since I moved my wife's bed into this room. Had it been a long-ago premonition that had us install a floor-length window that gave onto the middle-distance harbour and – way beyond – the eastern edge of the high moor?

Alice had always joked that, with her maiden name of Winter, by marrying a man called Summers, she was therefore fully entitled to introduce us to new friends as *The Seasons.* I don't think either family quite saw the joke, but it gave her many a laugh and was fully in keeping with her perpetual joy-of-life. The newly-installed enlarged view, she then had claimed, gave us a raison-d'être for our puzzling joint nickname, and she had enthusiastically set up her studio here to observe the passing scene. Her single concession to 'normality' being that a protective plastic sheet was allowed over the end of the sick-bed next to her easel.

The ever-changing, yet curious constancy in view evoked the achievement of a full life as the tide of hers ebbed rapidly away. Towards the end, sleepless by night and day, Alice had absorbed the distant energy as if preparing for a re-birth.

One of her last amusements may have been when an early winter's gale tore down our neighbour's overbearing, boastful trellis and scattered its matchwood to oblivion. Despite our mild protests, he had intruded on her view, but at the moment of its destruction, her grip on my grieving hand had taken on an old, long-neglected strength. Like mischievous conspirators we had grinned at each other; she had lived to see victory.

And now barely three months after the funeral I am being counselled to look anew at my own surroundings. I understand the intended purpose, but doubt whether the view would give solace.

So, what do I see this afternoon? The detail is dissolving and re-forming, as banks of hostile rain sweep across from the west; it is December, after all. A red fishing boat, rolling heavily at the harbour entrance, looks relieved to have made it that far. Seagulls have only to spread their wings and are instantly a couple of feet upwards; the unwary young, tails to the wind, pitch forward onto their beaks. Yet in the lee of my garden shed a blackbird tosses leaf with head-cocked unconcern. All else is a thrashing wetness that meets my mood today. But I know, and hold fast in my misery, that a delivery to be made this afternoon may cause the sun to shine again.

On cue, the doorbell rings and there is Alice's artistic mentor – or was it the other way round? He is gruff in his manly sympathy and meets my eye directly without embarrassment.

I won't come in,' he announces. 'Here it is, I think you'll like it.' And he hands over a flat parcel that needs two hands to hold safely.

'Thanks, Joe. What do I owe you?'

'Nothing at all . . . on the house . . . it's been a

privilege.'

And I take in the package; I know what it is. But beneath the discarded wrapping, the skill and craftsmanship of the mount and framing causes tears to spring anew.

It is, I believe, Alice's last work; I am fairly certain of this. She was surprisingly private about her ability, but here I have a vivid watercolour interpretation of our – no – her view.

Framed by Joe's extraordinary skill, a fleet of cloud ferocity assails the eye, small boats struggle to survive, even the two-dimensional neighbour's fence leans in dismay. And yet, in the top right-hand corner of the scene there is a hint of light breaking through. A water-logged sun that promises Spring will come.

I will hang the work on the wall facing the window. Then by looking at the scene outside and then at what Alice saw, I will be comforted by her presence.

Entranced, humbled and at peace, I seek her signature. She had always added a title to that, and there it was:

Winter's Window
Seasons 2010.

·····

The Twelfth Night Cake

Anita Langham

Cutting the Kitzel cake was the grand finale of The Empire Palace Players' year. When Walter Kitzel, pastry cook turned actor, died in 1812, his will included a bequest to buy wine and a Twelfth Night cake for the Players. Every year since then, it had been their tradition to gather in the green room after that night's performance, in full costume and make–up, for the ceremony of the Kitzel cake.

Fast forward to 1936 and the play was *Jack and the Beanstalk,* prompting some wag to conceal a bean in the cake – thus reviving the ancient custom of crowning the finder King of the Revels. But when one of the understudies discovered the bean, the merriment was not good–natured, for actors know how to titter cruelly. By rights, they whispered, it should have gone to Blaise Binney. He'd sown beans in a few gardens, hadn't he? Mainly belonging to young actresses. And him a family man, the cad.

Now when theatre folk party, they really party, so a hilarious Twelfth Night was had by all. But even this lot tired eventually so, leaving the spilt wine and cake crumbs for the cleaners, with costumes awry and make-up smudged, they staggered out through the stage door as dawn broke over the Empire Palace.

Nobody knew how long Sandrine had been on the Staff, any more than they knew how the theatre could function without her. Later that year, when rehearsals for *Careless Rapture* began, it just so happened that Zena Lane and her friend Dorothy Dixon visited Wardrobe for a costume fitting when Sandrine, whose needlework skills were legendary, was in there altering a beaded shift.

'Apparently,' Zena said, 'there's been rather a lot of careless rapture going on behind the scenes too.'

Dorothy giggled. 'Oh lawks! Don't tell me those jolly old beans've sprouted?'

They gossiped away, both ignoring Sandrine. In fact, like most of the company, they were in awe of her.

'She's like the scenery, darling,' they'd say carelessly if they were in a dark, shadowy area of the theatre. 'You only miss it if it isn't there, haha!'

They were braver beneath the bright light bulbs of their dressing-table mirrors. Then they'd whisper 'She's a witch...'

Sandrine, whose gimlet eyes were legendary, noticed many things. How nervous Miss Myrna Tutt was lately, how desperately she tried to conceal her expanding waistline. How much single malt Blaise Binney was getting down, how he was forgetting his lines. Which saddened her because, unlike some people, Blaise had always shown her unfailing kindness and respect. One night, Sandrine, whose prompting skills were legendary, rescued Blaise so often the Producer said she may as well go on and play his part herself. Afterwards, she knocked on his dressing room door and found Blaise still in make up, already well down a bottle.

'I've messed up, Sandrine...' he muttered.

'Which is why,' she told him, unwinding the silk scarf that shielded her tarot cards from malign influences, 'I've come to see what's to be done.' Shuffling the pack, she fanned it out in front of him.

'Don' bother tellin' my fortune... I know 'xactly what's goin'... to happen.'

'No you don't, ducks, but the card you draw will tell *me,*' said Sandrine, whose skills in divination were legendary. After some fumbling, he handed her a card. She turned it over. 'Number 12,' she mused, studying the picture of a man suspended upside down by one foot. 'The Hanged Man, eh? Interesting...'

'Wossat mean?' The drink was making Blaise querulous now.

'You've obviously suffered a setback, ducks, and it's turned your whole life upside down,' murmured Sandrine, whose psychoanalytic skills were legendary. You feel dissociated, helpless, isolated. You don't know which way to turn. Such a shame. Such a great talent wasted.'

'I've been such a... damned idiot, that's why, Sandrine. All I want is... to put things right... start all over.'

'I'm sure that can be arranged. I warn you though, you'll never be able to go back to your old ego-centred life. You're going to have to reconnect with your true self.'

'But– how?'

'Leave that with me – I see how it all fits together now. There's just one thing though, are you listening? Come hell or high water, you *must* get yourself to the Twelfth Night party – don't worry, I'll remind you, ducks.'

'How can you be sure it'll be January 5th?' Myrna asked, after Sandrine had examined her.

'Experience,' said Sandrine, whose midwifery skills were legendary.

'But– you'll miss the 12th Night party! Are you sure you won't mind?'

'No, no, I'll deliver the cake, then I'll come straight here and deliver your baby, of course I will. Don't you worry about a thing, sweetheart – that silly old party can take care of itself.'

'I can't tell you what a relief this is, Sandrine! I'm terrified of hospitals!'

In accordance with tradition, straight after the performance on the evening of January 5th, 1937, the company gathered in the green room, in full costume and make-up, for the ceremonial cutting of the Kitzel cake. The cake had been made by Sandrine, whose baking skills were legendary. It was voted the most spectacular show-stopper ever and, everyone agreed, she should be the one to cut it. She handed Blaise Binney the very first slice. He bit into it, pronounced it out of this world, took another bite then spat out a plump bean. Amid thunderous clapping and laughter, he was declared King of the Revels, a golden pasteboard crown was placed upon his head and nobody noticed when Sandrine handed the knife to Zena Lane and slipped out through the stage door.

Now when theatre folk party, they really party. Wine flowed freely, tongues wagged, tempers flared, accusations were flung – mostly by Merlin Tutt, a relative of Myrna, on his father's side. The quarrel culminated in Merlin snatching up the cake knife and rushing at Blaise Binney. Blaise, by then three sheets in the wind, his crown down over one eye, fled out into the passage, hotly pursued by Merlin, brandishing the knife and bellowing theatrically. Afterwards, nobody remembered why the pair climbed up into the flies, or, when Blaise lost his footing, how the cord became twisted around his ankle so that he hung upside down, suspended high above the stage. Or how long they all stood, heads thrown back, mouths open, too horrified, to move, to speak even, before the cord snapped and Blaise plunged head-first to his death.

At the exact same moment that Blaise's soul left his body, Sandrine held up a fine baby boy by one foot. 'Perfect!' she exclaimed, and, administering three smart slaps to tiny buttocks white with wax, red with blood, she spanked him into life. As the child opened his little gape and bawled lustily, Myrna smiled through her pain, sweat and tears.

'He's got a good pair of lungs on him - must take after his dad!

'Oh yes,' said Sandrine, I see a brilliant career on the stage for you, little man.' Then, laying the babe tenderly on his mother's breast, she reached for her scissors. As she bent to cut the cord, she murmured under her breath, 'And mind you don't mess up this time, ducks...'

.....

Iced Lollies for Breakfast

Maureen Taylor

'Mammy, will he come tonight?' we pestered, tucking into bed.
'You'll have to see. He comes if he wants to,' she said

Jack Frost paid a call as we slept soundly last night,
And today we woke up to such a pretty sight.

His icy breath silently left wondrous whorls,
Of swan's feathers, diamonds and fairy gown swirls

Etched on the glass, enchanting designs
We could examine them closely - they were on the inside

Our little red fingers scraped slivers of ice,
'Watch out! Don't get one in your eye!'

Tonight, we're prepared and we hope that he will
Cast his spell on the juice we've left on the sill.

.....

Winter Memories

Pat Atkinson

'Hi Soph, what're you doing today? Going out?'

'Yes, to the moon and back, what about you?'

Sophie continues, 'Have you looked outside yet this morning, snowing, blowing, icicles hanging from the gutters. You're unreal, Sylv.'

The identical twins had recently celebrated their 70th birthday.

Each had been through the work, marriage, children, work pattern of life and now Sylvia was divorced, Sophie widowed.

Taking the high ground as she was first born by 5 minutes before Sophie, Sylvia chirruped 'Cheer up, little sister, we can get through the worst that winter throws at us.'

She reminded Sophie of the days in their childhood when they had snowmen competitions, giving Dad the impossible task to choose the best. Recalling when they sledged down Branton Hill, tumbling off, deliberately rolling over and over to the bottom.

'Oh, if only we were those young girls again.'

'We can be, I'll give you an hour to come up with some more memories. Ring me later ok.'

'You come up with the craziest things Sylv.'

The resultant memories included igloo building, angel patterns, snowball fights, rolling giant snowballs.

Reality of how cold they were. Thawing out with steaming bowls of stew and dumplings.

.....

Winter Pantomime

Sarah Telfer

Inspired by Pablo Neruda's "Brief Poems" ("The Book of Questions", 1974)

what if forests disrobe for their winter performance?
showgirl their wood shaving legs while
backstage the button on pause for a spring finale?

what if dozy pines lounge with legs provocatively crossed
laughing at a beech as it fumbles to roll a
peppery bronze leaf for one last smoke?

what if oaks stand their ground in massive thigh boots
wait for their cue, dab at powder puffs of snow?

what if two sycamores discussing the weather
stride onto stage left in ivy gaiters
exit stage right their lines lost in memory fog?

what if a lonely robin is courted by a rowan tree
who, thinking the panto is done then shamefully plies
her old berries limp as bags of forgotten cherry lips?

from my seat in the balcony I see elms swaying to
the blackbird's song, hiding their nakedness with

tiller girls tawny owl feather boas
tittering magpies in the dark oh those
teddy boy brothel creeping bawdy jokes
throwing out he's behind you!

what if gulls endlessly snap from the circle like
paparazzi eager to awaken this shoot and that
their cameras trained on the inaction

what if I take root and tune into
snoring hedgehogs
a loop-de-loop squirrel that leaps
onto the descending curtain to steal
the final bow?

What then?

.....

POSTSCRIPT

The Seasons

Gabrielle Karimian

I love winter
Winter is the best
Just give me winter
And you can keep the rest

The cold the rain
The snow and ice
Grips the skin
In its savage vice

In the far north east
And the remotest reaches
In the city and the town
And the hills and beaches
It never disappoints or let's you down

Spring in all its glory
Is a different story
Of longer days
And dispirited strays
Of frozen bulbs

Summer attempts to revive
But can only provide
Distant memories
Of childhood times
And warmer climes
And melting ice creams
Are just fragments of dreams

Autumn arrives as it always does
Hung on the leaves of russet and brown
And branches hanging down
To cover the grass with its seasonal frown

So I will settle for winter
The harshness
The darkness.
But for every reason
Is the one reliable season

.....

Northumbria Region u3a Creative Writers' Group

Contributors

Alwyn Bathan
Anita Langham
Caroline Davison
Cecilia Coulson
Edward Cartner
Gabrielle Karimian
Maureen Taylor
Pat Atkinson
Pauline Bennett
Sarah Telfer
Shirley Fall
Susan Willis
Valentine Short